Stranded!

by Jenny Alexander
illustrated by Chris Prout

Contents

PEARSON
Longman

Text © Jenny Alexander 2003
Series editors: Martin Coles and Christine Hall

PEARSON EDUCATION LIMITED
Edinburgh Gate
Harlow
Essex CM20 2JE
England

www.longman.co.uk

First published 2003
ISBN 0582 79615 6

Illustrated by Chris Prout

Printed in Great Britain by Scotprint, Haddington

The publishers' policy is to use paper manufactured from sustainable forests.

1 Ten Whole Days!

Don't you just love the way grown-ups arrange things without telling you and then expect you to be happy about it? The first thing I knew about Clare and Peter coming was when Mum asked me to tidy my room and help her to get the spare mattress out.

"What – they're staying?" I said.

"Yes, Joe. For ten whole days. Won't that be nice?"

"No!" I said. "It's the beginning of the holidays and I've got plans."

She didn't even bother to reply.

Some people know their cousins really well and see them all the time, but Vicky and I had only met ours once or twice at big family get-togethers like weddings. The last time had been Granny Pat's seventy-fifth birthday party a few years before. Vicky was only four then, so she probably didn't even remember. Mum and Auntie Jean had been expecting Peter and me to get on like a house on fire because we're both boys and we happen to be the same age, which was obviously mad. Getting on with someone isn't about how old you are, is it? It's about how much you've got in common, and how much Peter and I had in common was zero.

I chucked all my stray clothes into the bottom of the wardrobe and kicked everything else under the bed.

I was feeling really fed up, and it didn't help to know that Peter was probably feeling exactly the same. I decided to make a stand. I wasn't going to share my room with Peter; if I had to let him sleep in it, I would go out and sleep in the shed.

That maybe sounds worse than it is, because I quite often sleep out in the summer. We've got this concrete shed at the bottom of the garden that Mum and I painted a few years ago – green on the outside and white on the inside. It's got a stable door and a proper window with curtains that Mum made out of an old tablecloth. There's a rug on the floor and a saggy sofa bed, so it's quite comfortable. At night, we've got a special torch that looks like an old-fashioned lantern, and we hang it from a nail in the roof beam. Mum found it in a car boot sale last summer. That's where most of our stuff comes from. We haven't really had anything brand new since Dad left.

Tinks got all excited when she saw me moving my things out to the shed. She kept running round my ankles and jumping up. She likes to sleep out there as well, because it's the only time she ever gets to sleep on a bed. It's amazing how much heat that wiry little body can generate when it's curled up by your feet. Mum likes Tinks to sleep out there with me too, because she says Tinks would bark and wake everyone up if anything went wrong. Like what? Does she think that burglars are going to break in and nick the sofa?

Vicky wanted to sleep out too, but Mum wouldn't let her. She said it would look unfriendly if both of us moved out the minute Clare and Peter arrived. So, by the time their car drew up, Vicky was sulking in her room. Mum told me, "Get her down here right now, and tell her to wipe that scowl off her face!"

Auntie Jean and Uncle Simon didn't stay long because they had a plane to catch. Clare and Peter looked as if they had got the winning numbers and lost the lottery ticket. Normally, when their mum and dad went away, they stayed with friends down the road, but that had fallen through at the last minute. The friends down the road had a big house in the town like they did, with a computer in every room, TVs the size of cinema screens,

and two cars out the front. There, they would
have had ten days of going ice-skating and
bowling, checking out the town centre shops,
swimming at the local pool. Here … What *were*
they going to do here?

Our house is called Carter's Yard, and it's up a
long track half a mile from Umberly. Umberly is a
small village about five miles from Cold Clayton.
Cold Clayton is a small town about a million
miles from anything else at all. The house has got
a wide, broken concrete yard in front of it, with a
high wall along one side. There are several lean-to
sheds along the wall, which look as if they're

falling down, but they're actually quite
weatherproof. We store our logs and coal in one
and garden furniture in another. We've got our
bikes in the third shed, and half a dozen spare
bikes in the one at the end that either Mum got
cheap or were given to us, but they're still too big
for us at the moment.

The garden behind the house is more like a
field really. Mum doesn't like gardening much. She
weeds the beds beside the patio and lets nature do
the rest. The shed stands in the far corner, up to
its knees in grass.

Clare and Peter didn't say much when we

showed them around, but you could see what they were thinking. You could also see what Vicky was thinking, which was quite embarrassing. She followed them around like a lovesick puppy.

"Clare's sharing my room," she whispered to me. "And she's really old!"

I pointed out that Clare was actually only twelve, but in fact she seemed pretty old to me, too. She had blonde hair with a red strip down the front, and trendy little glasses with designer frames. She was at least six inches taller than me, and Peter was about the same height, but stocky, too. They made our house seem too small, like a pair of strapping heifers in a little rickety byre.

After tea, Clare and Peter went upstairs to unpack their things. Mum made Vicky stay in the kitchen with us to give them a bit of peace.

"What are we supposed to do with them for ten whole days?" I asked.

"Well, tomorrow – what about a bike ride?" Mum suggested. "We're bound to have some bikes that would fit them."

"We could take them to Car Boot Creek!" Vicky piped up.

"Where's Car Boot Creek?" asked Mum.

"It's a made-up place. We give different parts of the village pretend names when we're cycling round, don't we, Vicky?"

"Yes!"

Mum was busy wiping the table. Vicky looked at me and attempted a wink. She was not the best person I could think of to share a secret with.

2 Car Boot Creek

Mum dug out two bikes that were a perfect fit for
Clare and Peter. I thought they were going to stick
their noses up at them because they were a bit
rusty and old-fashioned. However, they seemed to
have got over the shock of being stuck in Umberly
for ten whole days, and perhaps they had decided
to make the best of it.

"Where shall we go?" Peter asked, getting on
his bike. As if there was any choice!

We cycled into the village. Tinks came too,
running along behind. She's very good on the lane
and if a car comes she'll always go to the side and
sit down.

Sometimes she gets out and wanders into the
village on her own, but everyone knows her so
they always bring her back.

First, we went a few times round the green. I
didn't think Peter and Clare would want to go on

the play equipment, though we have some wicked games of 'shipwreck' there sometimes when there are other kids about.

Then, we went down the alley behind the church and into the car park. I did some jumps over the traffic humps, and Peter started showing us some tricks he could do. He was really good.

But Clare got bored so we went on. Pretty soon we'd been down every track and path in Umberly, and Vicky said, "Can we go to Car Boot Creek now?"

I hadn't been planning to, because I thought Clare and Peter might tell, and then we'd be in trouble. Mum only lets us cycle in the village, and we're not supposed to go outside the thirty miles an hour speed limit signs in any direction except home. But we had all day ahead of us and I couldn't think of anything else to do. So we swore them to secrecy, and went.

I liked to think that Mum wouldn't actually mind us going along the track to the coast road, because there's never any traffic on it. I told myself the only reason I hadn't checked it with her was that I just hadn't got around to it. I felt a bit guilty when Vicky and I went down there on our own, but it was even worse taking Clare and Peter, too. I decided I would ask Mum if we could

go there as soon as we got back – there wouldn't be any need to mention that we had already been doing it on our own for months.

You can't really see the sea from the coast road because of the salt marshes, but you can smell it. I hoped Peter and Clare weren't expecting sandy beaches and amusement arcades. The tide was low, so all the water had drained out of the creeks and inlets, and the salt marshes stood in a sea of mud.

We cycled all the way to the bridge without seeing a single car. The river under the bridge was not much more than a trickle winding out across the mud flats towards the sea. At high tide the

water would be nearly up to the top of the bridge and the mud flats would be all covered over, except where the flat tops of the salt marsh stood above the surface of the water.

We call it Car Boot Creek because it's like a car boot sale – there's loads of stuff there, washed up by the tide, and though most of it is rubbish you sometimes find something really good. When we

went with Clare and Peter that day there was just the usual crop of plastic fish boxes, bits of wood and rubbish from boats.

"Look at that!" Vicky said, excitedly. "Isn't it the side of an old cooker?"

She was pointing to a sheet of white metal lying at an angle between the mud and the grassy bank below the bridge. I knew what she was thinking.

"We're just having a bike ride today," I said. "Just a bike ride."

Vicky pouted. "Yes, but ..." She decided to ignore me. "Do you want to see something great?" she asked Peter and Clare. Without waiting for an answer, she left her bike on the verge beside  the bridge and went across the grass to the edge of the mud. It's quite low there, although most of the banks are too high and steep for you to be able to get down to the mud.

Vicky pulled the metal sheet out of the mud, and tossed it a metre or so out from the edge.

"Watch me!" she said.

I cringed. She was trying to impress Clare and Peter, and she was going to embarrass us both.

Vicky stepped carefully onto the metal sheet and the mud oozed up all around it. "There's one! Look at that!" she yelled. "Can you see it?"

Peter and Clare dumped their bikes beside Vicky's and leaned over the bridge to get a better look. A big red crab was riding the wave of mud like a surfer, pushed up from his hiding place under the metal sheet.

"Ugh … that's gross!" Clare cried, running down to the edge of the verge to get a closer look.

Vicky stepped across onto a piece of driftwood and the mud squished up all around it. Two little crabs came sliding out from underneath. Clare squealed. "I want to have a go!"

She grabbed a blue plastic fish box from the heap of rubbish on the bank and dropped it into the mud. I thought she was going to fall in, because she didn't put her foot right in the middle and the fish box tipped, but she managed to balance herself. The mud squished up. Peter stepped onto the white metal sheet. Personally, if I had been wearing designer trainers I wouldn't have wanted to mess around in the mud. But I wasn't, so I did.

We had a competition to see who could get the biggest crab. I didn't have to tell Clare and Peter to try not to fall in, because it was pretty obvious what would happen if they did. But I did tell them not to go too far from the edge. You have to be careful in the creeks.

Suddenly, Peter had an idea. "We could make a row of floating stepping-stones!" he said. "We could go across … to there!" He pointed across the first stretch of mud to the nearest raised area of salt marsh. I was not happy about it. Vicky and I never went more than a few metres out onto the mud, so that if either of us got stuck the other one could get the rope from the coastguard's notice-board by the bridge.

I tried to put them off, but they wouldn't listen. While Peter stood on a piece of wood, Clare fetched another one and passed it to him. He tossed it a bit further out and stepped onto it. Clare brought a rusty tea tray, stepping out onto the first piece of wood to pass it to Peter. In this way, they got right across to the salt marsh and scrambled onto it. "Come on, you two!" he yelled back at us. "Don't be a couple of stick-in-the-muds!"

"Stay here, Vicky," I said. She immediately jumped onto the first piece of wood and stepped lightly across. Tinks started barking at her, running up and down on the grass verge. I groaned. "Stay here, Tinks," I said, as I set off across the mud. Tinks was either better at doing what she was told or else just more sensible, because she sat down on the bank. But she whined at me as if to say "Okay, but I'm really not happy about it!"

3 On the Marshes

Peter and Clare ran off across the salt marsh.
Somewhere ahead, a heron flew up. Vicky went
haring after them. The river was over to the left,
winding across the dark mud like a silver snake in
the sun. Some oystercatchers were digging for
worms and shellfish near the water, and the sharp
'peep, peep' of their call rang out across the
marsh. We were going further and further from
the road. We were going too far. I had to make
Clare and Peter turn back.

They stopped when they came to another
stretch of mud. There wasn't much debris out on
the marsh, so they couldn't make stepping-stones
again. Clare found a low point where they could
get down to the mud. "Look!" she said. "It's
covered in birds' footprints!"

"We shouldn't be out here,"
I said. "We've got to go back."
Nobody took any notice.

"The mud looks harder here," said
Peter. "The birds' footprints have hardly
sunk in at all. I bet it would hold our
weight, Clare. What do you think?"

"Are you mad?" I cried. But it was too
late. Peter had already stepped down onto
the mud. He only sank in a few inches.

"We can walk across this bit," he said.

Now Vicky was starting to look worried.
"Come back!" she said. "You shouldn't walk on
the mud."

But there was nothing we could do to stop
them. The two of us just had to stand and watch
as Peter and Clare picked their way across the
mud to the next raised section of marsh.

When they got there, they couldn't get up onto
it; the edge was too high and too slippery. I
thought they would come back. But they were
larking around, slipping and sliding on the mud,
grabbing hold of each other to stop themselves
from falling over.

"It's not safe!" I yelled. "Some of it's like
quicksand. Come back!"

They took no notice. They set off round the

edge of the marsh, looking for a way up onto it. We lost sight of them for a few minutes. Then we heard a scream.

"Stay here," I said to Vicky. I grabbed her by the top of the arms and made her look me in the eye. "I mean it, Vicky. Stay here."

I waited until I was sure she had got the message. Clare was shrieking for help. "I'm sinking! Do something! Peter, do something!"

Peter came back into sight. "It's Clare ..."

I was making my way towards him, trying to tread in their footprints, where I knew the mud had held firm.

Clare had sunk nearly up to her knees in mud. She couldn't lift her feet at all, and even if she had been able to, there was nowhere firm enough nearby for her to scramble out onto. She was

really panicking. "It feels horrible," she kept saying. "Get me out! I'm going to be buried alive!"

I couldn't go any nearer, so I tried to calm her down by talking to her. At first, she was making so much noise I couldn't get through to her at all. So I shouted as loud as I could, "*Keep still!*" Then, having got her attention, I said, "I think you've stopped sinking now. But you're going to need some help getting out."

She stood still for a minute. The mud settled round her legs just above the knee.

"Peter will stay here with you," I said. "I'm going back to get help."

I told Peter to keep talking to her, and to try and keep her calm. If she started thrashing around she might begin to sink again. "Stay here," I warned him. "Don't try to go any nearer."

He nodded. "Okay. But don't be long."

Vicky was waiting where I had left her. We ran back across the salt marsh together. "We can get the rope," she said. I didn't tell Vicky that Clare was too far out for the rope to be any good. I wanted to get her safely back to the road first, and then worry about what to do next.

We came to the driftwood stepping-stones on the last stretch of mud. I went first to test them. I made Vicky hold my hand, although normally she would refuse that kind of thing, saying "I'm not a baby!"

When we were half-way across we heard it, the seeping sound of the water rising, and we saw the bubbles pushing up through the surface of the mud. The tide! I hadn't noticed how long we had been messing about in the creek, and now the tide was coming in!

It wouldn't come with a crashing of waves like it does further up the coast; it would come quietly, spilling over the mud flats, sinking them suddenly.

Vicky knew what was happening as soon as I did.

"We've got to get the rope!" she said. "We've got to hurry."

Tinks was going crazy, running up and down to the shore as if she couldn't bear waiting a single minute more. I thought she was going to launch herself onto the mud. So did Vicky. "Stay back!" she yelled. All the time, we could hear the slow seep of the water rising around us.

We clambered up onto the grass verge. Vicky ran to the lifeguard board beside the bridge. She grabbed the float and shook the rope loose. I took it off her. "They're too far out for that," I said.

"And anyway, there isn't time." She snatched the float back.

"We can't just leave them there!" she said.

"Listen to me. The water's coming in too fast. If we try to go back out, we'll get cut off." Vicky was so wound up she could hardly stand still. I said, "We've got to stay calm and not panic." Just then, Clare screamed. She must have realised what was happening. The water would be rising through the mud, creeping up her legs. "What are you waiting for?" shouted Peter. He was up to his ankles in water, too.

"We've got to get help!" I yelled back.

I took Vicky by the shoulders. "You and Tinks stay here. Keep talking to Clare and Peter, so they know we're not abandoning them. I'm going to run to that house …" I pointed to the nearest house, a hundred yards down the road. "I'm going to get help."

"But what if there's nobody at home?" Vicky demanded. "Or what if they can't help?"

"We haven't got time to argue," I said. "Please Vicky, just stay here and don't do anything stupid. Okay?"

4 The Incoming Tide

I ran as fast as I could. Tinks was going mad behind me, Vicky was shouting to Clare and Peter, and Clare was still screaming, but pretty soon I couldn't hear anything except the blood pounding in my ears.

I got to the gate and fumbled with the catch. "Keep calm, don't panic," I kept telling myself, but my hands were shaking so much I couldn't open the gate. I dived through a hole in the hedge. I raced up the path and hammered on the front door with my fist. No one came.

I grabbed the door knocker and knocked really loudly. Then I looked in the front windows. I couldn't see anyone. I felt panic rising inside me like the tide. I thought I was going to be sick. "Keep calm, don't panic!"

I ran round the side of the house and found myself at the top of a long garden. Half-way down it, there was a woman doing some digging. When she saw me she looked really angry. "What do you think you're doing?" she demanded, marching towards me. A man came out the back door. I was almost too out of breath to speak.

"My cousins …" I gasped. "Stuck in the mud. Tide coming in …"

The man pushed past me and disappeared down the path beside the house. I followed him. The woman came after us. We stood at the roadside looking out across the creek. Most of the mud had disappeared under water. Several of the driftwood stepping stones had floated up and drifted free.

From this angle, we could see Clare and Peter way out from the shore. The creek was filling up. The water was already above Clare's waist.

"We haven't got time to call the coastguard," said the man. "Come on!"

The man and woman ran down to the bridge. They went so fast I could hardly keep up with them. There were several boats pulled up onto the grass on the landward side.

"Give us a hand here," the man said. Tinks was still barking like crazy on the far side of the river. We couldn't see her because she was down in the dip. We carried one of the boats across the road and down to the shore. We put it into the water.

The woman
got into the boat.
She fixed the oars while
the man got in. They turned the
boat and began to row out towards Peter and
Clare. It seemed like they were rowing for ages,
but it was probably only a few seconds before
they got to them.

Tinks was still barking furiously. I shouted at
her to stop. There was a moment of silence and
then she suddenly appeared on the bridge. She
came haring towards me, barking her head off
again. "I know, I know," I said, trying to calm her
down. "But they're going to be all right now.
Look!"

The people in the boat had reached Clare. They were struggling to haul her out of the water. I guessed the mud would be softer now and she wouldn't be stuck so fast, but they still seemed to be having a job getting her into the boat. Peter seemed closer than he had been, and I realised he was floating now, not standing with his feet on the bottom. He was moving towards the boat. By the time they finally got Clare on board, Peter was almost there.

They pulled Peter into the boat. But what was that? There was still something in the water. I screwed up my eyes, trying to see what it was. The man turned the boat so that the woman could reach out and scoop it up. It was a float.

Vicky! I had forgotten about Vicky! Surely she couldn't have been so stupid … I raced back over the bridge to the place where I had left her. She wasn't there.

5 Under the Water

Tinks ran past me to the edge of the bank and stood staring out to sea, barking her head off.

"My sister's gone!" I shouted to the couple in the boat. "I told her to stay here. She must have taken the float to them."

"She was over there a minute ago!" Peter shouted, pointing to the nearest section of salt marsh. The man turned the boat. He rowed a few metres towards the marsh and then stopped. "We can't see onto the marsh from here!" he yelled at me. "Can you see where she is?"

I went to the highest part of the bridge and climbed up onto the wall. I could see right across the marshes, but I couldn't see Vicky. Suddenly, Tinks leaped into the water and started swimming out. I shouted to the people in the boat that my dog was in the water and she seemed to know where Vicky was.

"We can't see the dog!" the woman yelled.
"Which direction is she going in?"

I pointed towards Tinks, and then I saw Vicky
way beyond her. She was in the water close to the
edge of the marsh. She must have fallen in. She
was trying to clamber out, but the edge was too
slippery and she kept falling back. She looked
exhausted.

"Over there!" I yelled. "Vicky's in the water!"

They brought the
boat around and
rowed fast along
the edge of the
marsh. "Okay," the
man shouted. "I can
see her now!"

Vicky seemed to
be completely
unaware of what was
going on. She tried
to pull herself out
again, but it was
a half-hearted
attempt and she slid
back under. She
disappeared beneath
the surface.

When they got close to where she was, the man
leaned out of the boat and lifted Vicky's head
clear of the water. Her body was as limp as a
dishrag as he hauled her over the side of the boat.
They started heading back towards the shore.

I yelled at Tinks to come back. "Come on,
Tinks. They've got her now!" Her small wiry head
was barely visible above the surface of the water,
but I could tell that she had heard me. "Here,
Tinks!" I yelled again. I wanted her to swim back
under her own steam, so the people in the boat
wouldn't lose precious moments trying to catch
her.

Tinks turned and started swimming back. Shouting encouragement to her all the time, I ran back to the place where we had launched the boat and waited. I couldn't see Vicky. She was lying in the bottom of the boat. As soon as they got near enough, the man threw me the rope and I pulled the boat in.

They carried Vicky up onto the grass and laid her down. I wanted to pick her up and shake her, and tell her how stupid she had been. I wanted to hug her and tell her I was proud of her because she had been so brave. But I just stood there, rooted to the spot, watching helplessly.

Tinks came ashore and shook herself hard, so the water sprayed up all around her.

"Keep the dog away!" the woman said. She opened Vicky's mouth to check her airways were clear.

I swept Tinks up off the ground, but she wriggled so much that I nearly dropped her again. I hung on tight to her. Clare and Peter stood, soaking wet and shivering, close by. I felt so angry, I couldn't even look at them. The woman started giving Vicky mouth-to-mouth.

"We need an ambulance!" I said.

Suddenly Tinks managed to wriggle free. She hit the ground running. As the woman raised her head to take a breath, Tinks pushed in and started licking Vicky's face. "Keep the dog away!" snapped the man. But then Vicky spluttered. She was breathing again … And so was I!

The man picked Vicky up. She looked okay, but very cold and shaky. He asked Peter and Clare if they could walk and they nodded; they were shivering so much they couldn't speak. We made our way back to the house. As soon as we got there, the woman called for an ambulance and the man fetched some dry clothes and blankets, and made some hot drinks. He asked me where we lived. I told him. He said, "You had better phone your mum."

Mum was already cross before I even told her where we were, because we had promised to be home for lunch. When I explained what had happened, the line went quiet.

Then she said, "I'm on my way," and put the phone down. No goodbye, no see you in a minute, no thank heavens you're all okay.

"She's on her way," I told the others.

Vicky pulled her blanket more tightly around her. "We're in trouble now," she said.

6 Off the Hook?

Vicky, Clare and Peter went in the ambulance.
Mum and I followed in the car. She gave me a
really hard time.

"You were supposed to be looking after your
cousins," she said. "And how could you let Vicky
go out onto the mud flats on her own? In fact, what
were you doing down there in the first place?"

It went on and on, all the way to the hospital. I
had never realised how far it was before.

"That's Car Boot Creek, isn't it? You lied to
me! How many times have you been messing
around down there when you should have been in
Umberly? I thought I could trust you, Joe. I can't
trust you at all!"

The ambulance pulled up in front of Accident
and Emergency, and Mum and I went to park the
car. Tinks was asleep on the back seat. She was
worn out. I thought we should take her for a

check- up too, but Mum said she'd be okay. I wasn't happy about leaving her in the car.

We found Peter, Clare and Vicky in separate cubicles waiting to see the doctor. I sat on a chair beside Vicky. Mum wanted me to go and keep the others company, but I refused.

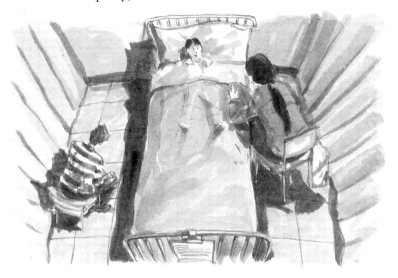

The doctor checked Peter and Clare over and said they could go home, but she wanted to keep Vicky in hospital overnight to make sure she was okay. That was what they always did when someone had been unconscious, she told us. Vicky was actually quite keen to stay, as she had never been in hospital before. Her friend Louise had told her you had ice cream with every meal and all the latest computer games in hospital, which had made Vicky feel she was missing out because she was just too healthy.

Mum could have stayed with Vicky, but Vicky didn't want her to. "I'm not a baby!" she said. So, once she was settled into the ward, the rest of us went home in the car.

Mum hardly said a word to me. Peter and Clare had a warm shower and changed into their own clothes. Then we had some hot buttered toast and tea.

I hadn't realised how hungry I was. Mum put a video on for Clare and Peter, and Tinks fell asleep on the sofa between them. Mum said to me, "You and I need to have a proper talk." I couldn't have agreed more.

We went into the kitchen. I sat at the table, but she stayed standing, leaning against the sink with her arms crossed over her chest. She was so angry with me, and it wasn't even my fault.

"It isn't fair, making me take all the blame," I said. "I wasn't the stupid one – they were. I tried to stop them, but they wouldn't listen."

"So was it their idea to go down to the creek then?" said Mum. "I don't think so. And I've thought all this time that Vicky would be safe going out on her bike with you."

I said I had never done anything with Vicky that wasn't safe. Cycling down to the creek was mostly along a track which never had any cars on it, and the coast road wasn't exactly a motorway. I said okay, we did go to the creek and we did play about at the edge of the mud. But there was no way I would ever go more than a few feet from the edge. Did she think I was crazy? The worst thing that could have happened was if one of us had slipped in the mud and got dirty. Actually, that had happened once or twice, and we had just washed the mud off our legs in the clear pool by the bridge. No harm done.

"I know I shouldn't have lied to you, and I'm

sorry," I said. "But I never did anything stupid, and nothing bad ever happened until today."

Just then, Peter and Clare came in. They must have heard us arguing. Peter said, "It wasn't Joe's fault, Auntie. It was ours."

"Yes, we were idiots," Clare agreed. "Joe told us it wasn't safe, and he kept asking us to come back, but we didn't take any notice."

Mum just stood there frowning at us. Had they said enough to get me off the hook?

Clare said, "We were all in a panic, but Joe kept a clear head. He knew what to do, and he was brilliant."

"We're really, really sorry," added Peter.

Mum went out into the garden without another word. I knew she needed time to cool down. I needed time to cool down too, and if Peter and Clare thought I was going to thank them for getting me off the hook, they had another think coming. I went out into the yard with my skateboard.

After a while, Mum came to see me. She said, "You were wrong to go outside the village without asking me first. I'm disappointed in you for that. But I'm proud of you for staying calm in a crisis." She touched my arm. "I'm really proud of you."

When she had gone inside, I went down to the shed and stretched out on the mattress. Peter and Clare came. They said they were sorry for getting in the way. "We knew you wouldn't want us to come. We knew you'd think we were just puny townies, not knowing how to climb trees and go fishing and other stuff like that …"

"Which we don't," agreed Clare. "I've never climbed a tree in my life."

"So probably," Peter said, "we might have been trying too hard to show we're not puny and we want to join in."

I gave this a few moments thought. "What, you've never climbed a tree?" I said. They shook their heads. "I've never slept in a shed either," said Peter.

"Yeah … well." If he thought he was going to sleep in the shed he had another think coming.

They went back up to the house. I stayed angry for a long time. But then I got to thinking. If they had never climbed a tree, they probably hadn't made a rope swing either, or built a secret den, or gone crabbing with bacon, or watched herons from a hide …

It would be a shame to stay angry for too long. We only had nine days left!